I0548267

Bolero Bird edition 2025
Copyright © 2025 Michael Whone
All Rights Reserved

Library and Archives of Canada
Whone, Michael
Mind the Bits: Notes of a Schizophrenic / Michael Whone
Bolero Bird 1st Edition
ISBN: 978-1-7753300-8-0
Book Design by River Van Style

www.bolerobird.ca

MIND THE BITS

Notes of a schizophrenic

Michael Whone

Portions of my previous book were written on a 300-Megahertz Tangerine Clamshell Apple iBook from the turn of the century; the book itself was written between the years 2019 and 2021. The reason for using the ancient iBook was because I was off my meds for half what happened and what I wrote in that book. The iBook required an Ethernet cord or Apple Airport card to connect to the internet, thus unwanted tracking of what I was writing would be impossible. My paranoia that the government was onto me overwhelmed me from one minute to the next.

The whole experience being off my meds is like being on LSD every waking hour, even when I'm stone sober. Since 2020, I've been on the Paliperidone injection every 28 days; a *28 Days Later* sort of story, ostensibly. I have no doubt that if you were to start a website, the CIA data centers in Virginia would crawl your site to check see if the content is of a dissident, however, I'm far from anarchic.

There are noticeable changes when coming off the stuff, but the changes aren't easy to deal with. The stuff completely alters brain function, so I wouldn't really notice much normalcy for six months, requiring I go through a period of nasty withdrawal symptoms, which then leads to a never-ending struggle to deny relapse into taking the drug again. Without the Paliperidone my mind is just a chaotic mess, full of pain and suffering. I feel it immediately every month, every 28 days, I see the nurse, I'm starting to feel the suffering, I get the injection and a wash of instant calm, a subtle veil of clarity shifts over me.

The whole thing that makes me tick, and pains my mind, is a plane, a mode of thought that appropriated my mind many years ago, and my only resistance to the ongoing threat is when I see the psychiatric team for a jab of the good stuff.

There's a bit of a pattern to the whole thing. This year is 2014-like in that the actual year is 2025, however a 2014 calendar works perfectly in 2025 too. I met a woman I loved on this day in 2014, and I've been expecting the pattern to repeat again this year. I met her on this day in 2014. She's been estranged since 2015, however, and married to another since 2021.

Furthermore, a few days ago I was checking out at the grocery store with a box of strawberry Pop Tarts, half asleep. "Sorry to wake you," the cashier says. Today I was checking out with a frozen Hawaiian pizza, and she looked at me smiling, all cutesy, "I'm not asleep this time," I said. Her facial expression had suggested I should say that.

Before that, I walked 4.5 kilometers in the morning. A woman detoured around where I was walking by on the sidewalk, holding up her cigarette to indicate that she didn't want to breathe her smoke at me. I pulled out my earbud and said, "I smoke. It doesn't matter to me." I smiled, she smiled, then she completely faced me, the direction I was headed and said, all cutesy, "Shouldn't I get a jewel in my crown for trying."

As I was leaving for the pizza a woman was there on the elevator. She had her dog, and she said, "At first she was interested in men, now she's interested in everyone." I didn't say anything. I walked 4 kilometers later in the evening and the same woman was back from walking her dog. "Were you out walking that whole time?" I asked. She hadn't been. "I like how she's so…" she said, as we went up the elevator. "Relaxed." I finished her sentence. "Ya, have a good night," she said.

I had the thought to start a book tonight, and I really have nothing to say anymore. I had hoped earlier today that I'd meet someone new on this Wednesday, Vimy Ridge Day in 2025, like I did on that memorable Wednesday, Vimy Ridge Day in 2014.

My previous girlfriend sent me a message and a video link before sitting down to write tonight. She broke her ankle and won't be able to walk for 3 months. The video was Miley Cyrus winning an award for the song W*recking Ball.* For some reason or other, a man got up and spoke about runaways and homeless youth, in place of an acceptance speech by Miley. "A dream you dream alone is only a dream, but a dream we dream together is a reality," the speech concluded. This award speech from May 2014 felt so long ago to me—but equally—so new, like new to my ex's son when he was little, but past its time in his new teenage world, hypothetically. This thought reminded me of waking up Saturday morning watching *Pee-wee's Playhouse* and eating the leftover salt in the bottom of Friday night's bag of pretzels because my parents hadn't woken yet. My life had just been beginning then, in 1986, (in a year that has a calendar that also works perfectly in 2014 and 2025) and had just begun again as I met that ostensible love of my life on Vimy Ridge Day in 2014.

The whole thing is a plane, based on patterns, and I had hoped my investments in the stock market hadn't crashed because of a Disney duck character, but this here is my beginning by some stretch of imagination. I'm not sure if this is going to be a book, but if so, that too would be a pattern that started in 2014. I'm on a new plane now, I'm not the book I was last. I'm eating the leftover salt, picking myself up from the hurt and pain of yesteryear, and feeling high on the pattern unfolding.

All of that was in the interim while a woman I've been talking to regularly went taciturn on me for a few days. She thanked me for the sentimental words I wrote to her, and I asked her if I was gay. I told her a guy yelled, "you're gay!" at me and then we were on hiatus it seemed. She called me this morning, and I thought everything was over, but she's still welcome.

I fasted most of the day because I was going to have pizza for supper at night. I usually find pizza to be overeating unless it's just a slice from a pizzeria, so all I had during the day was a Jamaican patty and a chocolate protein shake. I told this to the same woman later in the day and she told me, "You have to allow yourself some grace." Pizza for supper had been excessive, so I fasted most of the following day as well. Just a Jamaican patty in the morning, a chocolate protein shake for lunch, and two veggie wraps for supper and another Jamaican patty.

I've been thinking about the grace she suggested since she spoke of it to me. The thought was so sweet and non-judgmental that she seemed beautiful.

I went for a walk in the evening and a kid driving by in the back seat of a woman's SUV yelled at me, "Uranus smells like dog dish!" I could make out his words as *Paradise City* by Guns N Roses played at a low volume through my earbuds. I was almost home. The thing about that kid yelling at me, is that the first night I met the ostensible love of my life, the love interest in my first book, I walked her to her friend's house as we were closing the date. As we were arriving there, I hugged her and kissed her on the cheek, and a few teenagers drove by at that moment and yelled, "Hey fatty!" I think I listened to *I've Got a Feeling* by The Beatles after we parted on that Saturday April 12, 2014, the same day on the 2014 calendar as this year in 2025.

The next day I told the same woman that her comment about having a little grace was important to me and that I was moved by what she said, how the sentiment had been on my mind for a few days. She called me again in the morning and told me, "We have to build each other up, instead of being jealous." We spoke briefly again, and she said she was going for a walk on nearby trails in the woods today.

I want to step back a bit from the day to day and go a little backwards, although I think it's a little noticeable already that I have had a heel in the past already.

I've notably had very magical spring seasons for the past ten years, although in 2021 that whole magic thing took a major U-turn on me. I've been in a bit of a dance with the world, a bit of a *You do the Hokey Pokey and turn yourself around* kind of dance that's kept me beating to a different drummer from early on. Occasionally, the dance must come to an end.

Today is April 15th, but in March this year, the whole County had a huge ice storm that knocked out the power. The day that happened was the fourth Saturday of March. I looked back at my little blue notebook from when the magic was just starting to take flight. I had written a poem about the previous ice storm that struck our city, coincidentally on the fourth Saturday in March of 2016. I'll share the poem here; I'm not saying it's any good, I had been new to the literature life, starting out originally in music journalism, but the poem shows where my head was at during that time. By this point the dance had taken me great distances.

Mar. 27, 2016

I was inside
A woman
During the ice storm
last night.
The bed creaked

Outside the window
Tree branches snapped
and tumbled.

I've just been booted off the stage for attempting to say

the whole thing, because that sample just gets much worse from there. Although the poetry is autobiographical, I'm not in the place where I was then. That place worked for me then, and I continue searching for what will work for me on the plane I am now. I don't know what that will be; I feel I'm in another exposition stage of the dance and where the variations of the theme will go this time are completely uncharted.

The woman that has been calling regularly has been talking a lot about trails. I suspected she was implying some kind of subliminal *happy trails* statement because she hasn't been replying again for a few days.

The last time we spoke she said that she likes to visit Communist countries. I asked which ones, and I was surprised when she said Cuba because the word Communist felt so ominous, although I associate more positive feelings with Cuba, particularly. Unfolding this tidbit in such a way brought up an interesting contrast in moods for me that I felt an unlikely contentedness. I hadn't expressed that in response, but she went on to say that she's visiting Cuba with her mother in May.

I looked for the magic of April, the magic of the past hadn't just been in April, however, based on experience, this is where the exposition of the magic seems to appear. Jack Kerouac once wrote, "Will you love me in December as you do in May," which is a line from an old traditional song of Kerouac's senior. But as the criteria of the line suggests, I've always wondered if my April magic was a little too soon.

Ferlinghetti wrote in his poem from *A Coney Island of the Mind*: "The pennycandystore beyond the El/is where i first/fell in love/with unreality" The poem, soon after, concludes, "Outside the leaves were falling/and they cried/Too soon! too soon!" As this suggests, maybe everything is copacetic anyway, that it's *my* criteria that is *unreality*, that *too soon* is something of a constant in the mathematical way that the theory of relativity is, supposedly.

Perhaps May is too soon. The woman that I talk to regularly will be away in May, so I've the ultimatum of looking elsewhere or being too soon.

I had told the same woman that I wasn't looking to buy any new investments until June, or maybe even August, depending on timing. I suppose as subliminal as she's been, I've suggested I'm not ready to invest.

I went to the grocery story to buy a couple bottles of soda shortly after writing the previous bit. The price came to a little less than three dollars. I sort of fumbled my coins between my hands as I was making change and dropped two dollars. After handing the payment over to the cashier I looked around for the dropped cash but couldn't immediately spot it. "It's behind your heel," the next guy in line informed me. So, I put my left foot out to find the cash.

The past two days I've been *lost in the rain in Juarez, when it's Easter time too*, in a sense. The weather was nicer today, so I went out for a walk. There's no real plan where I walk, but I get around, which led me by my sister's old house, where she lived when my niece was born.

As I was walking by her house, I had the thought that perhaps when we die, the afterlife will return all my Karma to me, and I'll grow to be a mile tall. Then I had the thought that if I was a mile tall giant, I would incidentally knock a few things over, maybe even step on people like little insects. What would They do if that happened? Would They have to imprison me in a giant cell They built, or would I then be above the law, literally and figuratively? Would there be some unique giant woman who was a mile tall who'd been hurt all her little life who'd reclaimed all her Karma back too? Perhaps there'd be thousands—hundreds of thousands—of giant women that could play giant games with me.

None of us giants ever *put on any airs on Rue Morgue Avenue*, in our little lives. I know I never did. Is that worth any Karma in the end?

Then I walked past a construction zone. *This street is always under construction*, I thought. There was a guy with a dog taking his groceries out of his car into his house. The dog had been barking to suggest he was at his guard dog post as potential danger was passing. There was another guy with a dog who seemed like he was just starting out on a walk. As I passed by one of the front loaders on the side of the road, I noticed the guy with the dog was with an extremely beautiful woman who had face paint on that made her look like a corpse, and she had on all black clothes adorned with a few dangling silver chains.

Sometimes the strangest of things happen. In my first book, I wrote about a woman I thought I'd never hear from again. Over twenty years ago I met with her during winter break from college. I expressed to her the difficulty I had in continuing talking to her. I hadn't the words to explain fully. I said that she should contact me when we were in our 40s. I said that she'd probably be married by then, I doubted that I would.

She was married when she contacted me online last, a year ago. We spoke almost every day through the spring.

I suppose the future seemed too uncertain when we had split ways, too chaotic for me to keep up with someone that had no reason to be in my future. I had to search for a future that was on my terms, a future that was meant for me. I had struggled to see that any of my life was meant for me.

Margaret Atwood, in her book, *Power Politics*, wrote: "You fit into me/like a hook into an eye." The coincidence of that poem in my life is that I decided on a title for my first book when I read a copy of a poetry book by Irving Layton from a used bookstore. I found the Margaret Atwood book on the same day and took both home with me.

I mailed the Margaret Atwood book to a fellow writer

after reading it. I told her the words were too much for me. I had just begun my abstaining the Paliperidone at the time and didn't realize that the withdrawals from the drug were having a majorly negative effect on me.

The thing about that writer friend is that I spent the night in her bed once while she slept elsewhere. I slept in that room a few times; each time the tenant renting the room was a different person. That room seems to be a bit of a nexus for me.

I stayed there once while the room was rented by a guy that had a nice record collection. For several nights, while he was away, before I was prescribed a medical treatment, I listened to the U2 album, *The Joshua Tree*, on his turntable repeatedly for hours. I remember my sister owned that album on compact disc when I was younger.

When I was finally admitted to the psychiatric unit and given medication for my illness, I lay in the hospital bed with my old Discman listening and re-listening to my sister's copy of that U2 album that she owned growing up.

I've meant to deliver this story somehow for many years. I would have liked to work it into the first chapter of my first book, but it didn't fit in any way; and that poet friend was the first person I sent my book to after its release.

The memory of the nexus, the memory: so still and so unlively. I'm so confused thinking of the memory. I remember there was an old Model T era hubcap in the room at one point when I was there listening to the vinyl records. When my poet friend lived there, the dresser had dozens of books of feminist literature on the top.

At the beginning of this book, I said that being off the medications is like being on LSD for me, but that night in that room, in that feminist writer's room, I felt the feeling for the first time, like I had been incorrect; all things broken and lost, and unfitting in a perfect way like a note out of key in a jazz solo that swings the tune into the next bit, almost imperceptibly necessary.

Then, one day ... Each day moves to the next, and each light fits like a pattern. And the pattern is a plane. Eventually nothing changes.

Last summer when that friend from long ago contacted me out of the blue, I had been looking at estate sales. I was particularly intrigued by a set of speakers that were identical to the speakers my parents had with their Hi-Fi set when I was a kid. I purchased those speakers. I'm no audio equipment salesperson, but those speakers just seem to hit right. It's almost as if I'm listening to the present from the past.

I also took some medication around the same time, that supposedly closes the synapses in the brain that trigger certain memories to dissuade toxic behavior. I was a little skeptical at first, however I did try the stuff, and right on cue, I started having memories from around the time when all the toxic behaviors were in exposition phase. I had thought of that old friend who contacted me, while I was on the medical treatment, someone I never really thought I'd remember ever again. Then she contacted me.

I'm thinking of starting that medical treatment again this summer. I think there's potential for more improvement on top of the improvement that occurred last year. Who knows who might contact me if I start that up again?

I'm glad I never really got into the really debilitating

toxic behavior out there. I realized early on that I had quite an addicting personality, so I declined a lot of the toxic substance options out there. And now I think, people have such a hard time abstaining, and becomes a disease, but the real choice is right at the beginning, when you've never been on the stuff before. Once you start, then you never have the choice to not be a user anymore, you only have the choice to become recovering. This is really an important psychological choice people have.

My previous girlfriend is attempting to recover. Things seemed to have withered away with that woman that had been regularly calling me. My previous girlfriend still is locked to her bed with a broken ankle in a basement apartment with 29 steps to get up to ground level. She sent me a message that made me grin a little, as I was almost home from a walk the other night.

There was a couple of women with a man just exiting a car in a wealthy residential neighborhood. The man looked at me and said something to his company, and I believe they chose to walk past the house that had been their destination, because I looked back after I was already past them, and they were walking back to the house they passed as I was walked by them. "Let's talk about you and me. Let's talk about all the good things, and the bad things that may be," she wrote in her text message. Grinning, the moment had passed.

The next day a woman I connected with on a dating site called me a *scrub*. The moment had passed, and

I've updated my photos on the site again. I try to keep them up to date, because after you've been on there and never meet anyone, the photos previously used become out of date, and partially for transparency purposes, but also, preservation, I like to not seem like I'm living in the past. This seems like a notable feature of middle age and middle age crises: the tidbit of regression that surfaces in people I meet who are around my age.

Another thing I like to do is make sure I keep up to date with new music releases and try to de-saturate the amount of time spent watching old reruns. I think this is why a host of new genres are gaining in popularity these days, like true crime shows as one example: because the old reruns that have been playing for over 20 years are starting to date people that grew up on them, and they no longer want those ideas and planes, despite being addictingly familiar with them.

I'm familiar with a couple cones that pump out the tunes, but the tunes are fresh. I suppose it's difficult to restrict the regressive behavior a little more when you must have empathy for children in the house, and the schema of childhood one remembers is from around the time the Berlin wall came down or when Kurt Cobain died. I've never been on that plane, and I likely never will.

How bad am I? I mean, even Forrest Gump had a kid. I have to say, I read *Forrest Gump* when I was in grade school, and in someways a lot of the material I write is somewhat regressive in the sense that what I'm writing about is something of a dodo Forrest Gump vibe. All though the stuff I'm writing is clearly (meta also) fairly salt of the earth, it's peppered with higher vibes that are beyond that. Although, as it stands today, *Forrest Gump*, the creative work, has been an inspiration, despite being one of those passé things of yesteryear; could just be another delusional dodo thought of mine: my so-called life.

I used to get such a high from writing these little bits. Although, they started out longer than the bits I'm sharing here. Then I'd need to write even longer bits to get the high to new heights. Kerouac said in a *Paris Review* interview many years ago that he'd write for stretches of upwards of 8000 words or more in one sitting. He's such a unique character in the gamut of literature that I can't compare with that on any spectrum. I think if I wrote a section of 8000 words or more, I'd experience highs, then lows, and perhaps back to a certain height. I think the function of that for him had more to do with spending less time working and more time living, although that's simply speculation on my part.

Now I write these in slight bits only to diminish the high from it, the high off my own mind. There's a Radiohead song called *Nude* that goes: "Don't get any big ideas/They're not gonna happen." That song was written before I started my first book, and it's a song that is coming from a place of great experience as per my knowledge of the history of Radiohead prior to the song's release. I find myself in a more experienced place in my life where I also don't want to get high off my own thoughts and just maintain a level of balance that I can work with.

I used to walk around a plan, scheme, brainstorm, rehearse, jog all my thoughts repetitively and disciplined to come to the page to write a section that was overly thought out in hopes that someone would *get it* one day. And all of this would crescendo into the high as I was able to finish the lengthy bit, releasing from my mind all that I had rehearsed, documenting all that I believed was great and giant. And I simply don't want to do that anymore.

I could say that no one *gets it*, like I'm somehow noteworthy or what I've written is special, like some narcissistic self-promotion, however, that's simply not the case. Realistically, remaining balanced is better for me this way. I find this easier to write a little bit here on a whim, take a chance, and not feel a high off myself as I did in the past.

A friend I've connected with in the past recently shared with her social media that celebrities have become too much to themselves, making them clowns to the typical person out there. A new world of celebrity is on the brink, a new breed of public digestion is being brewed for us all. Despite being described here in my own words, the woman I know who brought this up today is a very brilliant individual. It's impossible for me to transmit this fact, but my respect for her is up there: more so than a lot of people who are typically revered in the public eye.

And maybe this whole bit is nothing in a sense that I'm unable to communicate the point perfectly well, rehearsed, painstakingly thought out, at the expense of being a narcissistic joke who's completely high off his own fumes. Alex Turner from Arctic Monkeys has a song from a few years ago that's oozing gorgeousness out my cones sometimes, and it goes: "I had big ideas/The band were so excited/The kind you'd rather not share over the phone/But now, the orchestra's got us all surrounded/And I cannot for the life of me remember how they go." The big idea, the big reveal that I can now tacit out from with grace, like I'm trendy.

That last section segues nicely into another *strange meadow lark*. That strange meadow is jazz school.

College reading week had begun, and Coldplay was the hottest new thing, there were no women in my jazz guitar class. The guy with the cool vinyl record collection and the U2 record that got me through had a Coldplay live DVD on the television in the living room. "They're hot right now," he said. "The ladies love him."

I couldn't for the life of me find someone who primarily listened to jazz and that's been a whole chaotic wild goose chase of a trip since leaving High School.

When I first started playing music, my buddy let me borrow his instrument. I took the guitar home with me and learned a few songs from the memory of what they sounded like. I didn't really have a lot of my own records to use as reference back then, mostly preferred the music videos on television that I could emulate while they were on the air at the time, rather than the radio.

I got my hands on some Beatles sheet music through my grade school music teacher, and our group of tyke music cronies were marveled. My buddy came to me and asked, "Do you know how to play a Gsus?" None of us had known. We took the sheet music to our friend whose dad played guitar. His dad was extremely cool: he had the

Jerry Garcia guitar, although none of us knew that at the time. The phrase, Grateful Dead, sounds too morbid for the typical twelve-year-old.

I found out later, turns out Paul McCartney tells the same story of trying to figure out what a Gsus is in a few interviews.

I had a cheap consumer-grade microphone that my mom had bought at Radio Shack before we had a compact disc player in the house. And we had two cassette players in the house at the time. I wrote some cliché 90s beginner guitar riff and recorded it onto one cassette recorder. Then I played the riff back on the first cassette player as I recorded a second guitar part onto the other cassette recorder. It was a primitive multi-track recording process.

I found out later, turns out the singer in The Foo Fighters said that same story as a keynote speaker at a SXSW gathering about a decade ago.

Everybody knows. We all did it, we all share a common story, a story that all the grown-up tyke music cronies get. We all know the story: you study music all your life, then you get to jazz school and learn the names of the jazz songs that famous hip hop artists used as samples in their songs. It's unfair to beleaguer jazz music and its hope to humanity continually brought to audiences worldwide every day. Although, for me, where I am in the world, there isn't much hope for me to pursue such esoteric alchemy. I truly believe in jazz, I really do. I have no place in that world though, and I had been on a road without a destination for many years after coming to this realization. Now I've become expansively hip to a plethora of new *block-rockin' beats*.

I found out later, turns out there's a myriad of similar stories from people around the world where there aren't jazz clubs on every block, and people who listen to sophisticated music like audiences once did. This *strange meadow* is just another esoteric music meme somewhere out there on the world wide web.

The day after watching the Coldplay live concert recording, my buddy's housemate went to work in the morning. Both were out and I had the house to myself. I needed to go out for a walk, but I was in an unfamiliar city, far from home.

I set out on the long road without a destination, strange meadows to the left and the right, unlike the cones I'd become familiar with till then. I found a convenience store, and was starved for anything, for nothing to change. I had no money; wasn't sure I knew my buddies' phone number or where they lived when I wanted to come back to my dissipation from home and mind.

I dialed a number.

"I'm lost. I don't know where you live," I said.

"I think you'll find it," he said.

I put my finger in the coin return to see if anyone left anything. My money was there. I only put in fifteen cents. The line had gone through, yet I hadn't paid anything for the call.

I headed anywhere towards nothing changing and the answer was *blowin' in the wind*, but the trees weren't swaying along. The world looked like a cartoon, and I was some two-dimensional caricature, although I felt one-dimensional.

I found the house, and the police came looking for me the next day at the front door. "Your parents are worried where you are," the officer said. "I'm right here," I said, although, that was a lie. "Call your parents and let them know where you are," the officer instructed.

I sent them a message in a bottle.

The ostensible love of my life in my first book sang into the bottle like the way you'd blow into a flute: "I'm going back to 505." The calendar in 2003 when I sent that message in a bottle can be used perfectly in 2014 when she sang that Arctic Monkeys song into the bottle that night at the playground in the cool Autumn night. "It sounds cool. What if I sang like that at the show?" kidding, she said.

She sang the song into the microphone for the audience and together we felt the dizzying light of the night's thousand eyes. The moment passed.

A decade passed.

It's a Monday, it's so mundane.

Perhaps I should call the woman who'd been calling regularly until a few days ago.

"I hope that someone gets my/I hope that someone gets my/I hope that someone gets my/Message—"

BEEP

For two days now the weather inside the apartment has been warm enough for shorts and a t-shirt. The weather outside is slightly chillier and is still hoodie weather. I remember going to Chicago to perform music with a jazz band in May: I came back from that trip completely sunburned. The weather in these parts doesn't get quite that hot until July. Despite the cold weather for about 3.5 months in the winter, all things considered, the weather around here is veritably splendid. Just over 15 years ago, I moved a little farther south from a city that was a degree of latitude below the subarctic.

With the humidity rising, the beard had been uncomfortable, so I shaved all my facial hair last night. I hadn't seen what my facial bone structure looked like in over a year, particularly near the jaw, and my face looked unusual. I love how there are many movie scenes that romanticize a man shaving his facial hair. In this way, something that is so mundane, so quotidian, can be thought of as moving to others. Those scenes typically give the impression that this is a man being stripped down, like taking turpentine to a used canvas and going back to *carte blanche*.

My previous girlfriend sent me a message. "We might be neighbors," she said. She's still nursing the broken ankle in her basement apartment. Perhaps she was able to find a better place. We had been looking for a place to share while we were together. At one point she invited me to move in with her in her current apartment.

If she does move nearby, I will be excited. Although, I'm stuck on the anticipation of getting my injection in a few days. This month hasn't brought me too much of the withdrawal symptoms as this medication cycle is coming to an end. The last time I was with the psychiatric team, I said to them that things typically go better for me through the month when I have people to talk to regularly.

In many ways, the women that talk to me most days are incredibly important to me. Filling the air with words that mean nothing, over the phone and in text messages, means everything to me; like little grammatical rations that bring sustenance from one day to the next.

Every day, when the weather is nice, I spend much of my time on the balcony looking at the people passing by on the busy street. The balcony faces a gas station on the other side of the road. In the morning, a woman comes by with her dog to talk to a lady who meets her standing out on her second-floor balcony. The dog is so well behaved that he's always unleashed, doesn't bark and always seems to know what's going on. Sometimes I walk by their conversations and the dog looks at me with an expression of understanding in his eyes.

A long time ago, my dad had a model of a futuristic gas station, with all the pumps and overhead shelter. None of the gas stations at that time looked like that. There's a certain kind of beauty about a gas station; in that they are the heart of most long-distance travel. A car as a social construct or social concept is nothing without the gas station. Sometimes I see pictures of gas stations, out in the barren desert, with cacti in the background and plateaus, and the scenery says so much about the meaning of driving and travelling around by car, all fueled by what the gas station provides.

Now the gas station across the street looks exactly like that old futuristic model. Back then, I never would have thought a gas station would look like that, like something out of a sci-fi movie. And now that I'm living in the future that some sci-fi writer a long time ago told us was inevitable, everything seems as plain as day; classic.

Even the thought of tablets and smartphones seems to have crept inconspicuously into our lives as well. I remember seeing the young college students on buses who used tablets and there had always been something pompous about using those. *I never want to look like one of the people,* I thought. And slowly over time, this just became a natural feature of the world we live in. Anything that isn't extravagant, and beyond its time seems oddly out of place in the world that completely sticks out like a sore thumb compared to the rest of the content in the history book.

In this way, those old rundown desert gas stations I look at in pictures are more appealing to me than all the opulence taken for granted that I see from day to day. Now, everything seems like a joke that had been designed to imply we're progressing, headed towards good things, that there had been some kind of plan all along.

And one day, when all the people who understand that the future is now are all gone, we will be left with a bunch of architecture and designs of things that no longer have any implied meaning. None of the architecture and designs are going to have any cultural significance to any of us anymore. The cars themselves are all starting to look futuristic to someone who lived when John Lennon died or for others who lived before that, yet these designs are completely meaningless to most of the people who typically make use of them. To some people, this just *is the way it is*, however, if they looked closely, there's more. There's so much more if you listen and pay attention.

Sometimes people tell me I look like a famous person, some guy or other that's in show biz. Ricky Gervais a few times. Now that I've shaved, I look even more like him. A guy I used to work with thematically told me to be like Michael, confusing the American version of *The Office* for the British version. In *The Office* the British version, Ricky Gervais plays the same role as the American Michael character but is named David Brent. The whole bit from my co-worker was just like the show itself.

Once, I was wearing aviator glasses and a guy told me I looked like Mark David Chapman. Chapman wasn't famous per se, he went down in utter infamy, but he has his own Wikipedia page, and I'm not too far away from going down in (non-violent) infamy myself.

I had a friend who was an editor of Wikipedia, he saw me performing with a jazz band at a club, so he tried to get me on the list of famous jazz musicians. My name stayed up on the Wikipedia list for about a day and half. So, technically I was a famous jazz musician for a little less than 48 hours. Yes, somehow Wikipedia makes the whole thing legit.

That woman who contacted me after more than twenty years suggested to me that I try manifesting what I was looking for. She said she understood that she had no place in my *end game,* but I should seek to be the person that would attract what I'm looking for.

My thoughts on manifesting remain unchanged. I feel as though if you drastically alter who you are, your thought process, appearance, behaviors to attract someone, and eventually once you've found what you are looking for, you will slowly transition back into who you really are, and then the person who you've attracted will not recognize you as the person they had originally fallen for. In this sense, I believe that the concept of manifesting is most likely a way of describing a manipulation tactic derived from self-promotion.

The whole idea lends itself to the thought that people are of no real substance and should be taken only by skin-deep description.

My first girlfriend told me she once had breast implants, but they had fallen out. She told me she used to be extremely tall because of stints she had in her legs. She also told me she would fit clothes sized 0. None of this was true but there was something about all of these lies that said something about what *she* thought mattered to people. The whole thing is a slippery slope because we become accustomed to change, so something of a change eventually becomes nothing, nothing is ever enough, and as such we are prone to creating change that effectively is for the worst.

Most people want nothing to eventually change, but without patience at the core of our values, we innately do things for the sake of the fact that we can. It's like saying there's no sense in investing money for the future, saving for a rainy day, because we have money and what we do with money is spend it. What else is the purpose of money?

I need nothing, because without nothing there's only nothing: no something. Nothing is really the basis of all value in this sense, so the true market of desirability is not really defined by the influencers, and the glamorous magazine ads and billboards. True value is defined by the constant of the existence of nothing. This is why I'm of no matter to others, because what I say and do does not represent the core definition of value.

This does not make me less important in anyway, only identifies the point that what I say is slightly novel because there is no nothing of me to eventually change, to amplify all that is valued in the world. But, for some reason, Some people will view my schizophrenia as a feature of marginalization, despite that no one would notice if I did not tell them. Even so, all the deconstructed bits of me are novel: nothing more, nothing less, naturally.

Roberta Flack sang: "Possession is the motivation/ Hangin' up the whole damn nation/Looks like we always end up in a rut/Tryin' to make it real, but compared to what?"

The last time I was at the doctor, he says, "There's nothing about you that would make anyone think differently about you." I'd like to be different in some way, somehow special, but I will never be that. I blend in like a piece of chewing gum that lost all its flavor. What is noticeably negative at times is my own attitude of myself. It seems no one else shares these opinions.

I remember I had just been diagnosed with schizophrenia in my early 20s. I wanted to get back into reading and I had no other place to turn around and start a new book than Kerouac. The feeling I previously had reading Kerouac was very good for me; I'd read *On the Road* and *Maggie Cassidy*.

I was at the bookstore pining *The Dharma Bums* on the shelf and had no money to buy it. I remembered a line from a section in *On the Road* that justifies the characters in the book stealing food in a grocery store on the West Coast. In the same vein, I used the line to justify taking that Kerouac book from the bookstore with no money, as a means of survival, as per the justification Kerouac lined up for me in his seminal work.

this	is.......	justified
here	a	margin
there	a....	margin
just	some	dharma
just	some...	bums
bum	some	dharma
dharma	some........	bums
full		disclosure
full		justification

One can only hope their morally bankrupt lines are justified. It appears my bum lines are kismet. Something's come up, I was having difficulty swallowing: everything's congruous, nothing is value, and this is all novel.

Originally, my medication for the schizophrenia was Zyprexa, Celexa, and Epival. I stayed on those three medications until 2014, at which point I was directed towards the injection I'm on now. The original medication had some strange side effects, one of which was like an electrical shock sensation that felt terrible. I didn't have much of a social life at that time, most of the people I knew consistently blew me off and gave me the cold shoulder. I didn't start to have much luck with the social life until I started on the Paliperidone injection in 2014.

Back when I was originally diagnosed, I would leave that nearly subarctic town and come back, leave, then come back. Almost every time I went back, the first person I'd run into there was a woman I went to school with who was a friend but liked to tease me. Oh brother, did she really tease me back then in High School. I'm still connected with her online, she lives out west now, and we've both had the benefit of maturing a great deal since those early days.

She recently started a new job making flower arrangements at a garden center. I described her as *the flower girl* from that old hippy song. The two of us agreed that because she's *the flower girl*, she's now a certified hippy, which, by association to her, makes me a hippy also.

Who knows what that entails at this stage of the game? We discussed the old bell-bottoms she wore to school, and the parties we had. She used to stay over after parties in a spare bed with her boyfriend at the time, then make breakfast for the three of us in the morning; something I found luxurious as I wasn't used to having someone around serving me a whole bunch growing up.

From what I understand, she's had some issues with mental illness in the past also. Like me, you'd never really notice any of that unless she informed you. The stuff is invisible to most people. What I do wonder is how many people who are on the spectrum of novel people will view the mental illness label of a person in a way that degrades them or discriminates them.

The woman who had been calling me regularly finally sent me a message to check in on me. I was already talking to a new woman on a dating site before that. She says she's been couch-surfing today. Similarly, I started out on CNN and soon hit the harder stuff. Yes, the hard-hitting in-depth journalistic look at myself again for nearly the second straight week.

I haven't told any of these women about my mental illness, and I wonder if they'll hold it against me if they are informed. I'm writing this hard stuff and it'll be out there, sticking out like a sore thumb to people who likely thought I was normal. However, I suppose at this point, saying that I'm abnormal is slightly convoluted because I've said already that I'm totally of the novel variety. This is the issue I see: the doctor says I'm no different, no one sees me as different, I don't get any special treatment in anyway, but as soon as I drop a bit or two about my medical treatment, there's some itchiness about me.

The whole thing is totally speculative anyway because unless someone says something, I don't really know what anyone is thinking, so I just go along hoping someone wants to connect in some lasting way, despite the social obstruction of the term schizophrenia for people.

I have a buddy that I used to talk to about music because he's a singer and somewhat of a music guru, relative to the sort of small-town flair of the place where we live. But he called me up when I was depressed and, in his words, he said: "You're a weirdo!"

It's just impossible to view yourself as others view you. The concept of trying to agree with how others view you becomes too convoluted to be healthy for anyone. I just do my thing, and if it comes across as some weird book, I can't worry about how the person reading the stuff thinks of me.

You just gotta, "Keep movin'. Keep movin' on," as Tom Petty sang. Never let anything bring you down, so I'm just getting excited for the release, because I feel the whole thing is turning into magic again, like Imagine Dragons sang: "I got this feeling in my soul/Go ahead and throw your stones/Cuz there's magic in my bones."

I didn't understand anything anyone was saying in kindergarten. I was enrolled in French immersion and the instructions didn't mean anything to me. The teacher told us that if we did something good, we'd get a star beside our names on a board at the front of the class. I never got a star.

We had to cut out some pictures and glue them onto a page. I used too much glue.

The teacher gave us percussion instruments to play along to some French recording on a vinyl record player. I didn't understand the song. They showed us the instruments one by one and named them all. Maracas, shakers, triangles, drumsticks. I got a cowbell beater, and the teacher was trying to tell me to use it like a washboard, but I could tell those weren't designed for that type of sound. I lost interest early on from that moment because the teacher didn't know what she was talking about, and the whole thing was like that right until the day I didn't go to school anymore.

One day this kid kept talking to me in French as we were waiting to go home, and everyone's just standing around waiting, I had become incredibly impatient, because the only thing keeping us standing in a huddled group like that near the exit was some erroneous rule that we had to be there until the bell rang at 3:15. If we didn't stand there like little automatons in production, the teacher wouldn't get her pay, so we were there for the benefit of the teacher who needed some erroneous job she couldn't do right. I lost interest in the whole thing early on, let me tell you.

So, as I say, this kid is talking to me in French, haven't got a clue what the guy is saying and I decide to knock him down, take him out. He had no idea what was going on, he thought the world was a sweet place. I knew it was garbage right from the start.

I failed kindergarten that day. I had to put up with another year of that nonsense.

By grade three, I would go to my locker before we were all carted off into the prison yard, grab my harmonica, put on my beanie with sides rolled up above my ears, and I'd toot a tune until we were shipped back in from the prison yard. People would be playing basketball, some throwing little pieces of glass at the wall, drawing chalk lines on the pavement, I'd toot my little tune.

I had a perfect score on my province-wide standardized test for that grade.

By grade six I was almost ready to be a contestant on *Jeopardy*, I would have been better off getting a job in some factory. I would have been better off in a factory than beleaguering my life with teaching me how to write things like this.

The teacher told me once that New York City was the capital of New York State, which I knew wasn't true. The teachers were always a little off, they were clearly there for a check, had no depth beyond the kind of facade you typically see on the nightly news.

I graduated grade school with the highest grades in the class.

40 years of schoolin' and they can't put you on the night shift.

My dad watches those singing competition shows a lot. Every time I visit, he puts on one of those shows. He also watches the talent competition shows. He tells me I should try out to be on them. I think he thinks I like that sort of thing because I'm a musician, but I very much detest those shows, even down to what people who watch those shows think good singing is.

For one, none of those people write their own music, which is most certainly a feature of someone who doesn't have a great deal of musicianship. People say that there aren't a lot of women in the Rock N Roll hall of fame, and this is evident of a gender bias. However, the first thing to note on this point is, which a lot of people are unaware of, many of the famous female singers that came about didn't write their own music. The women who were massively popular, but also wrote their own music, are in the Hall of Fame already. If there is a bias, it's not so much the discrepancy when giving credit where credit is due, it's in that the music industry of years past seemed to have felt that the messages of women in song were unsuitable for mainstream audiences.

The other thing I dislike about these competition shows is they seem to be stuck on one style of singing that supposedly is deemed good. However, when my dad listens to music, he doesn't listen to that style of music. So, there's this disconnect between what mass audiences are told is good and what different groups of people are saying. I personally find the singing on those shows incredibly annoying, for the most part. As much as people say Bob Dylan can't sing, or many others who are considered songwriters who are bad singers, usually I'd rather listen to them than some singer that's supposedly the greatest. I must dismiss the idea that a lot of people have that the most technically proficient musical performance is always the best.

Many of the alternative artists from the 90s became increasingly popular simply by way of the fact that beginner guitar players could easily learn the songs that they had recorded. When you went over to a friend's house, and he started to play his acoustic guitar, inevitably, you'd hear a Nirvana riff or two, or a Weezer riff. What sold a lot of those songs to all the little guitar tyke cronies out there was the simplicity of those tracks. Furthermore, much of the popular music I hear on the radio these days can be boiled down to a common denominator of a 2 to 4 chord harmony construct. Even the Beatles didn't write songs like that, other than the songs that were based on the blues. This is just to say that there is a pervasive unmusical plane that's influencing thought on music, in which, typically, musicians don't particularly ascribe to.

In this sense, connecting with people who know very little about music, for me, can be a bit of a challenge, because much of the opinions of music that people hold are simple baseless of any kind of musicality. The only people I seem to really connect with these days seems to be the musicians I know who are out there keeping the music world alive.

Like, has anyone read *Rolling Stone* in a while? It's a music magazine that is no longer centered on music. I have a subscription through Apple though, I love it, and am a long-time reader, however, the articles have no backing on the level of a music scholar. As a musician, and music lover, you must pay into keeping current by reading about all the uninformed, baseless opinions of music that are trending. A magazine like *Downbeat* however, the long-time jazz journal, still is backed by musicality as a foundation of its views.

Aptly, this is just to say that I'm more likely to agree with the views of AC/DC, Prince, or Cher, than of these judges on these competition shows, or what's worse: the opinions the people who watch those competition shows. And if the option arose to visit a cartoon Duck character in the oval office to defecate on the desk, or watch a vocal competition show, the latter is *way* more cringe.

I told my mom that when my dad dies, she should get a dove as a pet because they're so elegant, beautiful, and sacred. The only caveat is that they drop little turdlings all over everything and everyone, so she'd have to train the dove not to do that to her. And then when people come over, she could have the dove perch on their hands. At first, they'd love it, but inevitably the dove would drop the little brown bee-bees on them. The guests would have no choice but to decline holding the dove for long, at which point my mom would then take the pet back on her hand, and as per the dove's training, she would say, "My darling dove doesn't do that to me, see? I'm perfect."

I used to go for coffee with my parents a few times a week. Slowly, over the last few years, doing this has become entirely unbearable. The instant my dad sits down to have a coffee he starts in with the complaints. If someone could pay a subscription fee to stand at a kiosk in which customer care agents took complaints all day long, my dad would be first in line for that service everyday. Anything and everything, you name it, my dad has some kind of complaint for that.

I can't fathom how my mom does it anymore. She's there with him for a coffee date everyday, and not so much as a peep about my dad's wicked complaining is heard from her. The whole concept of masculinity goes out the window in old age, I feel. At one point in his life, a man is the epitome of masculinity—all those cliché traits they describe men with—leadership, management, dominance. One day, as the docket gets closer and closer to judgment day, men lose all those traits only to become what they once painstakingly heeded as weakness—everything that's small and worthless—useless complaints, one after another. According to my calculations, I've only got a few good years left where I'm still anywhere near relevant to people, relatively.

The woman I was talking to on the dating site has

informed me that she had left a long-term relationship of 26 years. She says she's healing and growing. Then went on to say that she's in a process which helps her get in touch with lingering issues and enjoying solitude. The whole thing sounds like a euphemism for leaving a man that completely went AWOL from relevance to me. She's only 50 years old, too.

Jimmy Fallon's character in the famous 70s music journalism nostalgia flick, *Almost Famous*, is quoted as saying: "If you think Mick Jagger will still be out there trying to be a rock star at age fifty, then you are sadly, sadly mistaken." Then goes on to say: "You gotta take what you can, when you can, while you can—and you gotta do it now."

It's just an inevitable force of nature. The magic comes, and slowly dissipates more and more, until you can't squeeze together two rabbit feet for the life of you, and everything that mistakenly glances in your direction can't hide the disdain you evoke.

Old man, take a look at my life: I'll never be like that, I'll never be like that, I'll never be like that…

In 2001, I performed in the pit band for the theater production of the musical, *FAME*. There are some interesting guitar parts in that score. I remember doing the dress rehearsals on stage, everything went fine. Then came the day of the first performance for an audience. The stage director told me I couldn't wear the clothes I was wearing on stage. Anyone who wasn't in the cast had to be wearing all black.

In those days I was pretty broke all the time, and I've never really been overly concerned about appearance, so I didn't have a lot of clothes to choose from. My only pair of black pants had a hole in the crotch, and I really had no money for a new pair of pants. So, I went ahead and wore my only black pants. The stage director didn't like that, and what's more: I was a guitar player who had no black clothes. What in the world is a guy with no black clothes doing playing guitar? How bizarre.

On my first ever music gig, I wore a pair of brown dress pants, a light brown collared shirt, and a pair of dapper brown Clark's shoes. I envisioned Ed Bickert, the famous jazz guitarist wearing something like that in his heydays. I even had the Fender Telecaster affixed with a Gibson 57 Classic humbucker swapped in place of the standard Tele lipstick. I almost went down to see one of

Bickert's last shows before he retired, but I was waiting for some jazz vinyl records to come in the mail from New York City, and I didn't go. Turns out one of the trains that could have got me there that weekend ended up crashing. I spent the weekend listening to my Bill Evans *Montreux II* record on the turntable instead.

The only picture I have of myself in action as we performed *FAME* for that show run, I could see my red underwear showing between my legs. The antics got me in with some of the cast members, who referred to me as the *hot* guitar player, behind my back. I never thought I'd be going to cast parties in my life, as a guitarist, but aside from my memories of the love interest in my first book, I think being a part of that theater production was my second-most favorite time in my life, hopefully more times like that to come.

My previous girlfriend sent me a message confirming that she has secured arrangements for moving into her new apartment where we will be neighbors. She was extremely excited and mentioned how we will do all kinds of things together. She's moving mid-May.

The messages from her seem a little forward. I haven't seen her in over eight months. I can't remember if we said we were still together. We might have, I don't remember. I will be neighborly with her once she's nearby though. I like her, she's a nice person, and showed a significant interest in me when there was no one else. I'm happy for the correspondence we have together.

She also said that she will be going for her cast on the same day I go for my injection. So, I could run into her at the hospital while I'm there. She also said she's staying with her father, since she's unable to get up the 29 steps to the front of her apartment, and her dad had thought to get her a wheelchair during her recovery.

I'm hoping this all goes smoothly for her, and that she does well in physiotherapy after she gets her cast off three months later.

The interesting thing about her is she used to be a television personality when she was in her early 20s. She did a television segment in which she would go out onto the street on a live broadcast and conduct short interviews with people there. She's even dated some semi-famous musicians in the past. I found her impressive when we met, but she's very private, and mostly keeps to herself and her kids as she's become more mature.

I know another woman like that who works for a popular morning show in the big time. I went to a party at her summer house over 20 years ago. There were lots of people there, and she had a tremendous vinyl record collection. I was jealous of all the hip original pressings of Stones and Led Zeppelin records there, to name a few of the highlights.

There was a well-known punk band performing for a little while, but they seemed like they'd rather join the party than perform, so they only played one short set that I luckily caught the tail end of when I arrived. I guess that night was a great time too, but hardly enters my mind. I struck up a conversation with the guitarist and he showed me some of his rig that he had been using. He had a beautiful black Custom Shop Les Paul that I couldn't fathom ever being able to afford in those days.

I used to run around with this tall, beautiful blonde girl when we were in High School. We used to go to the mall with friends and then sneak off and kiss near loading docks where people wouldn't catch us. We spent about six weeks together. I don't really refer to her as my first girlfriend because looking back at a relationship with a teenager is a little cringe to me now, but I used to see her every Friday night when the school weeks ended.

When we stopped seeing each other, I moved my guitar lessons to Fridays and my parents started taking me to see the local jazz musicians perform at a restaurant. I loved it, all the musicians were great. Sometimes we'd go on Saturday afternoons and there was a jazz guitarist with an upright bassist. Both could really play. I didn't know much about what they were doing at the time, I just knew I liked the sounds they were making.

After I left jazz school in my 20s, I played in a jazz jam where I met one of those guys that performed in some of those gigs I saw with my parents when I was in High School. Then from there I got the two of us some gigs at a bar called *Envy*.

I had already set up on the stage and I went down to the street to wait for him. He pulled up in a van that could easily be used for touring. He grabbed his bag of cables and amplifier out of the back and said: "You carry the holy grail." He was referring to his 1965 cherry sunburst Gibson ES-175. The whole gig, the zeitgeist of being there and feeling a slice of the energy that originally moved me to study guitar so deeply was there at that time. I performed that night with a Rickenbacker Sierra, which is now a discontinued model by that guitar manufacturer.

Another guy I met recently has asked me to perform at a jazz jam in town next week. However, I'm not sure I'm up to the challenge anymore. I have a nice Gretsch archtop, with some jazzy flat-wound strings, that doesn't get much play anymore these days, but I don't really feel motivated to participate. There's something about the way things are going in the world, and the energy I feel from modern music and musicians that keeps me away from doing that kind of style. I feel disconnected from that world somehow now, and lot of the disconnectedness has to do with spending so much time with women who were so far from any semblance of a stake in that world, and my energies have taken a similar circuitry to go along with them.

Something comes up like this jazz jam like a blast from my past, and I feel I'm putting myself out there for women in a way that contorts where I should naturally be, the energies that should flow in and out of me fluently. However, I'm not there at all, and I feel more potential with the energy I do have where I truly am.

July 28, 2024

Producer grabs control room mic
Such energy
Funkier

The eyes in the booth:
Funkier?
how?

At the piano:
Funkier than
a mosquito's tweeter

Happy Easter how are you?

I'm not sold on this last bit I wrote.

Imma think about it.

It's kinda obscure.

A little tainted

I'm not sure.

Listening to music though.

Enjoying

That is very groovy

Twas

The women that I had been closest with fell into a slight pattern. They either had an older sister, or a father with the same name as me. I typically found women with a brother ruder towards men, particularly if she had a younger brother.

The other pattern I noticed is that the women I was close with all became successful in their lives. They all did well, and I do believe that my influence had a big part in how their attitude towards life led them to their success. I can't take credit for any of this, other than speculatively, but I do have a good track record for having strong feelings for women who made something of themselves. A lot of the women I met were quite unstable before I was through with them, so I attribute my positive influence on at least a large part of the closeness of us.

If the women that did fall hard into somewhat of a despair after we were through, it had to do with a certain type of chasing of declination as a mode of being or plane they had been on. In those cases, I was unable to really be all that great to them other than to walk away. But also, I don't think the pursuit of declination could ever bring them the kind of person that would do them any good. I couldn't change attitudes like that. On the whole, the women in my life had displayed a great deal of resilience.

Likely, my presence and being had frightened them straight, towards the thoughts that they could perceptibly wind up permanently crook'd like me, stuck and rutted.

I had been researching in the library for an essay on *The Catcher in the Rye* when a guy from my grade 12 math class approached me.

"Do you know what this is?" he asked.

"It's a pipe."

"Sixty-nine!"

The wooden pipe was carved to fashion two bodies entwined and astride one another in carnal delight.

Better Get It In Your Soul

So **much** depends
upon

thirty-two bars
repeated

vibin' to the soul
got **hit**

chorus *after*
chorus

I didn't call too many tunes. The tenor-man called most of the tunes; it was really his band. Technically, the band belonged to the drummer; he was the most technical. Technically, I was the most technical, but I didn't sound that way, which is what I've always been going for anyway.

I called *Willow Weep For Me*.

"You play the head," the tenor-man said. "I'm used to hearing it with the tag that Dexter Gordon does."

Anytime I called a tune Dexter Gordon was known to play, our tenor-man would refuse to play the head. "What's with you? You wouldn't play Scrapple from the Apple because Dexter plays it different than Parker. You know Dexter's version and Parker's version both fit with the changes."

"I just don't like Dexter Gordon very much."

"This is news to me. Why not?"

The tenor-man grumbled and turned away.

"A tenor-man who doesn't like Dexter Gordon. I thought I heard everything. You know, you can play Parker's version the first time through the A section, and Gordon's version the second time through and it'll sound like a call and response."

"I'm not taking a solo. You guys play."

"Okay, let's play something else then."

"No, you guys do it."

"Alright, I'm ready."

The pianist started off with the last eight bars as an intro, the drummer was in with the brushes and upright bassist with a half-time beat at the top, as I took the head.

The tenor-man didn't take a solo and he called in a sub at the next gig. For our tenor man astray, we had a chuckle conspiring to play the Dexter Gordon tag when we played *Willow Weep For Me.*

She was a religious deity, and I think I'm the only one who celebrates her sacred soul. I hold ceremonies late at night in my room, where I line up to hold the chalice that commemorates her brilliant love, and then I repeat the ceremony, hundreds of times, until I feel a stupor that prevents me from thinking of her anymore—I have what seems to be an addiction to libations in celebration of her. Why was she sacred?

She loved me—was too bad that I didn't know how to love her back.

As a result of my habit of conducting libationary celebrations in my room, I've become depressed. So, I gave her up a few weeks ago. I substituted her with another. Apparently, she is also a depressant, but I'm not totally convinced of that. There's been a difficulty to be extremely depressed when all you feel like doing is looking in the mirror, watching yourself hold your tongue with your head cocked sideways for hours at a time, even though this only had been a minute that passed.

I'm convinced that by looking directly into the lights above my mirror, that they will burn a lime green colored decal into the dull brown colors of my eyes. Though, when I'm not holding her near and dear, I'm a little skeptical that this is going to work.

"Let me see."

I was embarrassed but I turned around and lifted my shirt.

"Yes, I see. I can prescribe something. You live alone; I suppose you don't have anyone to rub on a topical."

The neighborhood was pretty run down, one of my few friends would call it *sketch*. The pharmacy next-door looked like a front. Seventeen dollars for the script was doable on a guitar instructor's pay. I didn't know I would have a reaction.

Watching the cars enter the parking garage across the street entertained me. I felt like learning French, picking up and heading to the capital. The timing had to be perfect, right after a car entered the garage. I could see what the parking garage looked like from the inside. I would look at the inside of the apartment from across the street. And I took up running. There were real runners that shook their heads at impostors like me. I couldn't make it around the track behind the public school down the street. I needed the best shoes, the kind you see on Nike commercials. One of my students looks like a teenage doppelganger of my *sketch* girlfriend.

Another guy was a writer with a 647 number and was infinitely cooler than me. She liked him more; I was sure of it. Surely, he had no acne on his back. How could she love a young man too insecure to take off his shirt. Luckily, the lake is too polluted for swimming. One of my students looks like a teenage doppelganger of Nina Simone, she didn't like swimming either. I felt better with her; she liked learning about jazz. The *sketch* teen gave my skin a reaction that went away after my lessons that night. I was embarrassed that my shoes looked like clown shoes. How could someone under six feet have such big feet?

The roses started talking to me. The next day the roses had burned. I suppose the water I sprayed on them helped them to burn. I wasn't an avant gardener; jazz is dead, isn't it? Wynton Marsalis came to town and blew my mind. I mean I felt like my head exploded, blown apart by a trumpet. I couldn't decide where to eat. Everything was fattening, and I felt guilty after eating fast food nuggets. How do I sound more avant garde? Is there a special scale for that? Was my teacher hitting on me when he bought me a drink after his set? I was just there to see if Wynton Marsalis would stop by a little, run-down jazz club in the city. I *knew* he would! My teacher must have been on top of the world, getting schooled by Wynton.

In between lessons, I drank water and inhaled deities for the voice. I was developing a great rasp to sing with. There was a time of no calories in the aspartame. So healthy, could never be thin enough. I wondered what that junk would taste like. I felt like tasting the junk. Surely,

I've tasted it by accident before, but I wondered what my junk tasted like. What was the flavor like?

I went in my pill bottle. I thought about tasting the junk again but couldn't bring myself to try. I held the bottle to my mouth but put the cap back on before that stuff reached my mouth.

I read *French in 24 hours* by the pool. The rain came down and I lost interest before 24 hours ticked by. People who read Robert Louis Stephenson are smart. Reading *The Strange Case of Dr. Jekyll and Mr. Hyde* would impress my *sketch* girlfriend. I must be smart because I'm ugly. Only eating two pieces of the pizza will make me skinny, and hot to my *sketch* girlfriend. I just threw out the rest of the pizza, so that wouldn't go to my hips.

She never calls me.

I should visit her anyway. I mailed her a birthday present wrapped in newspaper. Maybe she still has the book I sent her, and she'll kiss me for it. It was so clever to wrap the gift in a newspaper. Who does that? Circling all the instances of her initials on the newspaper, I must be a genius or something.

One of the cars in the parking garage had the top down and keys left in the ignition. They left the car specifically for me to use, I know they want me to see my *sketch* girlfriend. If I go as fast as I can, they won't even notice the car had been missing.

I put exactly $5.23 in to replenish the tank. I once called my *sketch* girlfriend at 5:23 PM because I told her

I'd call her at 6, and I couldn't wait long enough to call her again, so I decided I'd call her 30 minutes before 6, but not exactly at 5:30 because that would look like I was waiting until an exact time to call her. 5:23 was the magic number, because it made me look like I wasn't trying too hard but was totally stoked to talk to her. I want her to know I like her.

There was a police car parked at the intersection just before the parking garage. I slowed down when I saw the cop there. I stopped at the red light. The light turned green and I went through. My balmy hands slipped on the wheel as I was about to turn into the parking garage and the cop lights went on.

Whoop Whoop!

I pressed the button on the visor and parked the car next to a Porsche. My *sketch* girlfriend would probably think I was cooler if I had a Porsche. Maybe if I had a Porsche parked outside her door next time, she would answer.

lit as the ***on air*** sign
the radio *silence*
is *intense*

When I was 18 years old, I had a gig through the summer, three nights a week. There was a small pay after each night, and I could also receive tips from patrons of the bar. The stint also included a free dinner each night I played. I had the same menu option each time, something that was called a Triple Decker BBQ Pita, which was probably one of the most delicious things I ate all year on the little amount of money I had at the time.

The dinner was a chopped, grilled chicken breast with BBQ sauce, and tomato, lettuce, alfalfa, bacon slices, held together between three miniature naans. That was a couple of firsts for me, the first time I had both naan and alfalfa. I was marveled by the naan bread, and didn't know what it was until about a decade ago.

After each night, my buddies came to see the tail end of the show, and we'd go out on the town together.

"That's a cool car. I wonder what kind of car that is?"

"It's an old MG."

"The logo looks like Mercedes-Benz."

"No, it's an MG, like Booker T and the MGs."

"You sure?"

"*Seriously.*

"You know, Green Onions? You know...

"*Na-na... na-Na Na na-na. Na-na... na-Na Na na-na.*"

Out on the **night** street
young and wild
sad and *ecstatic*
breaking rules like **squares**

And the music I played was nothing to awe about, I never really did anything all that amazing; nothing exceptional as The Barenaked Ladies who—disappointingly for the music industry—never won an award for inspiring the creation of pre-cooked bacon long ago, the key ingredient in creating my favorite meal effortlessly, the Triple Decker BBQ Pita; a treat meal and a memory every now and then, now that I know how to find the naan myself. However each meal seems to be more and more square as time goes on, and the rules seem more unbreakable because anything I desire to do is done rightly within the lines.

A sound does not exist. The sounds that we hear are each made up of a number of different sounds. There cannot be a sound without sounds.

The excruciatingly beautiful matter of sounds, the hearing of co-existing subliminal definition, is the inherent entanglement embedded within, even to the very marrow of its existence.

Trading Floor

everyone has
stories

entanglement was
our gatekeeper

for trading them
like *currency*

In 2002-2003 I used to visit a woman in her dorm every weekend. At one point in the year, she began using an erasable marker to write little sayings and things on her wall. I lay on her bed and read the inscriptions that had been there. For a month, I thought of the perfect thing to write. I pondered. Finally, one day: "Can I write something?" I asked. She handed me the marker.

Eventually nothing changes

I thought she would erase my contribution, but the bit remained. I had been 20 years old, and she began asking me, thematically, as the year went on: "*How are you doing in your retirement?*"

A guy who slept nightly in the gas station across the street in the winter before the 20s snuck up on me early in the morning as I was waiting for the bus. "Is anything ever going to change?" he asked, startling me.

I talked to a woman on a dating site tonight:

How goes the online dating?

> Nothing ever happens. It's just
> a distraction mainly. Seems
> like anyway.

I don't feel particularly
romantic or sexy ever anyway.
The whole thing makes you
kinda hardened.

**Yea I'm not sure what to think. I
just signed back up yesterday.
Nothing ever changes.**

You said more than the other
people already. lol

Really?!

You seem like you have a little
bit of energy.

You're a "live one" by
comparison.

I haven't played guitar in 59 days. I don't really feel like playing at all for the time being. I'm sure I will play guitar sometime soon, but it's been a while. I still listen to a lot of music though. At the end of the year, my streaming app informed me that I listened to 80,000 minutes of music in 2024. That's over 55 whole days spent listening to music.

I mentioned to the woman who's been calling me regularly that I think if I ever made it with any of the music I've released, I wouldn't really want to go out there and perform on a tour or something. I don't even envision myself ever going out and doing that. I'm 40 now, so the idea that I *could* is somewhat of a longshot, but even still, when I was going strong in music, at a much younger age, I don't think I ever really had the intention of making a career out of performing.

I think that is one of the most crucial things in converting just another guitar player into someone who goes out and makes it. To be successful, the musician must feel an untamed desire and need to go out and perform for people. Unless the musician has that desire, the chances of making it are going to be diminished significantly.

If the desire is there, though, the chances of making it are improved incredibly. This is speaking speculatively;

however, the successful musician requires this passion, not just the passion for practicing.

When I was talking to her, she mentioned Mick Jagger does it at his age. I said: "That guy loves going out there and perfoming people. He woudn't rather do anything else in the world. That's what that song is about, in my opinion." The fact at hand isn't totally my age that's preventing me from going out and grabbing the reigns of whatever career here that might be available.

At every show, Mick Jagger sings, "No sweeping exits or off-stage lines/could make me feel bitter or treat you unkind/Wild Horses couldn't drag me away"

Everyone thinks of the famous Rolling Stones song, *Wild Horses,* as some undying love song, but one could easily interpret it as a whole-hearted passion for a performer's audience, and love for standing up and delivering the goods to said audience, night after night, despite any other opportunity that may arise.

When I had more energy to play music, there were many things that I didn't have going for me. A minimal level of talent and knowledge was there, I feel, but things like funds for proper equipment, funds for transportation and rehearsal spaces were all beyond the rationale of my being a musician, realistically. Thus, the drive and passion to go out and play had no medium to build within myself, and instead I looked for other opportunities that seemed slightly more within my reach.

In any event, I haven't got much longer to go in my 28-

day cycle. I could see how the despair would easily take me over after a while. I'm just trying to keep it cool as best as I can and enjoy the music I get to listen to because the listening and discovering the vast landscape of the industry still is important to me to as ever.

I still grow, although the growing now seems to be viewed externally as something of an overgrowth at my age, like nostril and ear hairs.

While I had been waiting for the nurse, I thought about two dozen times how close I was to ending it all. I didn't care anymore, there's no point. *Eventually nothing won't change.*

I was on a 12 hour fast before I went into the hospital for my blood work. After the lab technician took my blood, I finally had a bagel for breakfast with a coffee. I could sense the sad expression on my face, as I killed some time until my appointment with the med clinic. I had lost all hope.

After I ate, I slowly made my way over to the psychiatrist's office. I had arrived early for my appointment, but I was able to see the nurse without waiting too long. "Sorry I'm early," I said. "I wanted to do my blood work early so I didn't have to wait much longer for breakfast."

"I understand," the nurse said.

He took my vitals first. "Your vitals are perfect, even your breathing is like someone who works out a lot," he said. I mentioned that my diet was very good. "That could be it."

We discussed my difficulty keeping off the sweets. "Sometimes when I have a craving for sugar, I'll eat a 6-pack of butter tarts all at once," I said.

"That's not good."

We discussed the weather being not overly conducive to getting out for exercise. He asked if I go to the festivals in the summer. I said that I go, but that was a lie—I don't really. Whenever I go to one of those festivals that the city hosts, all I see are couples with their families, and the vibes just heighten my loneliness. I've been alone all my life, and there never really was any glimmer of hope to meet anyone.

"Invega, 100 milligrams," he said. "What's your birth date?"

"Right arm today," he said.

He walked over to my seat. I had my sleeve pulled up onto my shoulder. "Just a little poke."

He shot the Paliperidone into the muscle in my arm, and that was all I needed to make everything alright. Uncontrollably, I felt a wave of release in an instant.

I didn't see the doctor at this visit, but I walked by him in his office and I sent a cheerful hand wave his way.

"See ya!" he said

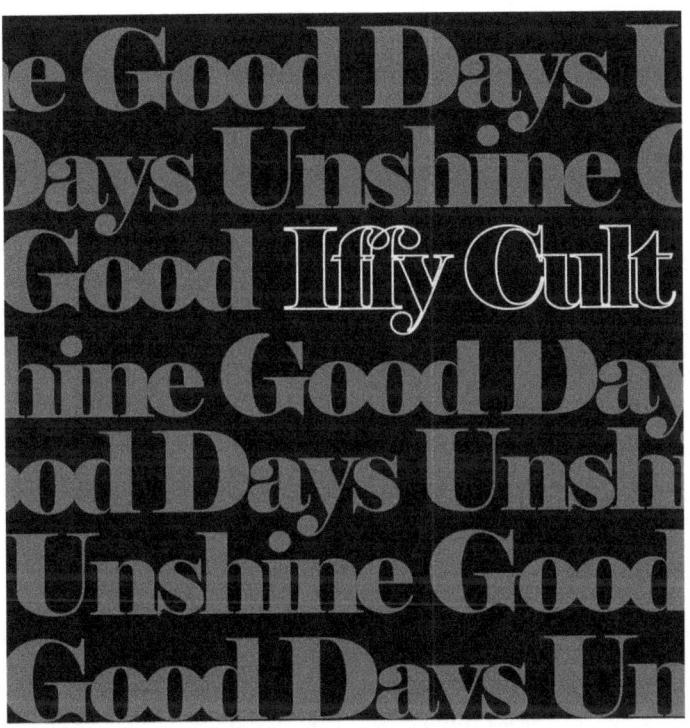

Discover the New **IFFY CULT** album
GOOD DAYS UNSHINE
NOW ON VINYL